Ruined

Addictive Crime Suspense Political Thriller

Andi Easton Series
Book 1

Ava S. King

304 publishing Company

Copyright © 2022 by Ava S. King

All rights reserved.

No part of this book may be reproduced in any form or by any electronic or mechanical means, including information storage and retrieval systems, without written permission from the author, except for the use of brief quotations in a book review.

This is a work of fiction. Names, characters, places, and incidents are either the product of the author's imagination or are used fictitiously, and any resemblance to actual persons, living or dead, business establishments, events, or locales is entirely coincidental.

For questions and comments about this book, please contact 304 Publishing at info@304publishing.com. Visit the official website at www.authoravasking.com

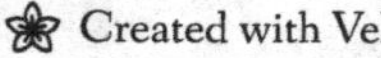 Created with Vellum

*I want to dedicate this book to my family and friends.
You are always with me, no matter where I go, and
everything you've taught me has made me a better person.*

Latest Releases: Ava S. King

Agent Red Fatal Memory Teagan Stone Book 1
Agent Red Fatal Target Teagan Stone Book 2
Agent Red Fatal Crime Teagan Stone Book 3
Agent Red Fatal Justice Teagan Stone Book 4
Agent Red Fatal Enemy Teagan Stone Book 5
Mirror of Lies - A Jessica Smith Book 1
Agent Red Fatal Death Teagan Stone Book 6
Mirror of Lust - A Jessica Smith Book 2
Ruined: Andi Easton Book 1
Upcoming Releases (2022/2023)
Agent Red Fatal Revenge Teagan Stone Book 7
Christina Harris Mystery/Thriller Series
Agent Red Fatal Pursuit Teagan Stone Book 8
Agent Red Fatal Attack Teagan Stone Book 9

Disclaimer

This work of fiction contains strong language and explicit content and is only intended for mature readers. The story may contain unconventional situations, language, and sexual encounters that may offend some readers. This book is for mature readers (18+).

Introduction

Synopsis

Andi is looking forward to a fun-filled night at her best friend's wedding. But when the newly minted analyst assigned to the Terrorist Threat Assessment Team arrives, her plans quickly unravel.

The bride's uncle, a longtime prominent senator, is kidnapped. Andi jumps into action to rescue him, but as she follows the clues, she discovers the victim has secrets —dark secrets that change everything.

Will she solve this baffling case before it's too late?

Chapter One

"You came!" Hilary jumped up from the chair and hugged Andi tightly.

Because of her new position, Andi had already informed her about her possible lateness for the rehearsal dinner. As the youngest member of the Terrorist Threat Assessment Team at the FBI, Andi Easton followed in the footsteps of her father, Jed, a police chief in Washington, DC, and brother, Aaron, who entered the army. Generations of helping the community lived in her heart. In Washington, DC, the Easton name was well known, but she was determined to succeed on her own.

But one person who didn't like her new role was Paula Easton, her mother. Besides Sunday family meals, she preferred not to deal with her mother, Paula. The tension grew every time she was in her presence, and snappy remarks went back and forth.

"I told you I might be late." Andi waved at Hilary's family members around the restaurant.

Andi became best friends with Hilary in high school one day during lunch, and they continued that friendship into college. Although most girls enjoyed partying and dating, Hilary and Andi focused on achieving their academic and professional goals.

Hilary, who stood a few inches shorter with a slim build, came from a generation of a political dynasty and carried it with pride. Hilary was an attractive woman with rosy skin, a round face, and oval-shaped eyes. Whitney, Andi's other friend she'd met two years ago—a twenty-eight-year-old with spunk and the comedian of the bunch—worked as a nurse. They'd have girls' nights every blue moon, but once Hilary got engaged, their schedules clashed.

"Andi, glad you could make it." Levi raised his arm around her shoulder for a hug.

Andi stepped around the table to kiss Hilary's parents, Marlin and Dee Hawthorn. They were her second parents, and she loved them dearly.

"I had a long day of paperwork." Andi sat down in the chair next to Hilary.

Their wedding would be a big event and feature in all the major newspapers. A few magazines and local TV stations even wanted to air the wedding ceremony. Levi came from a wealthy family with deep pockets in DC politics, and Hilary was a teacher who wasn't impressed with his money back in college. Somehow, he broke down her walls, and they became friends. Later, they dated, and now they were engaged.

"How is it going?" Hilary picked up the bottle of champagne and poured it into a glass.

Andi rested a hand on the table. "So far, it's paperwork and getting familiar with the staff and operations."

"So proud of you, Andi." Hilary covered her palm and squeezed.

Andi returned her squeeze. "Proud of you and can't wait for tomorrow."

Hilary leaned over and whispered, "Can you believe I'm about to be Mrs. Levi Baldwin?" She clinked glasses with Andi.

"No. I thought we'd be two old ladies sitting on the porch together." Andi chortled and gulped down the champagne.

Andi loved her best friend, but Hilary didn't have the best track record with dating. Each one disappointed her, from minor things like not paying for meals to significant issues like cheating. Andi had often thought they'd end up living together because Hilary was too set on perfection.

When the restaurant's doors opened, all eyes turned to the guest who arrived twenty minutes late. As Senator Ted Hawthorn entered, a flash of temper lighted Hilary's eyes. Andi's gaze followed him as he shook hands with onlookers and waved.

"I told him not to come if he would be late," Hilary hissed, putting on a fake smile when her uncle approached the table.

"Look at my beautiful niece." Ted cupped Hilary's face and pressed a kiss on her cheek.

Ted Hawthorn was known for making a show out of anything if invited. Hilary's uncle on her father's side was all about appearances and staying in power.

"You're late," Hilary replied, raising an eyebrow.

A hard gleam appeared on Ted's face before he grinned and released his grip. "Levi, I hear you've been doing well for yourself," he said, ignoring Hilary's admonishment.

"Mr. Hawthorn." Levi extended his hand to Ted.

"Mr. Hawthorn! Sorry, sir, you have a call." Their waitress motioned toward the phone held by the bartender.

A flicker of irritation and impatience shone in Ted's eyes. "Everyone knows I'm off the clock, but I guess the life of a senator never ends." A chuckle echoed from his chest, and he turned to walk toward the bar, taking the phone in his grip.

Andi placed the napkin on the table, tapping Hilary on the shoulder. "I need to run to the restroom."

She walked out of the private dining area and passed the bar on her path to the bathroom. Andi pushed the stall door open and sat, quickly finishing her business. Once she flushed, washed, and scanned over her makeup, she went to the door. She gripped the knob to open it and noticed a spot on her shoes.

Someone cried out in pain on the other side of the door, and Andi jerked it wide. The hallway was empty. She glowered. The door to the men's bathroom opened, and a guy walked out.

Andi lifted a hand. "Excuse me, did you hear something weird a minute ago?"

"Like what?" His brows blended together.

"I don't know. Maybe someone was hurt."

"Sorry, I didn't see anything." He shrugged and sauntered back to his table.

"Andi! Andi!" Hilary motioned for her to come back to the dinner table.

"Maybe I'm hearing things." Andi laughed to herself and strolled back to the party, taking her seat.

"All right, we're going to finish the night with a big thank you to everyone who came," Hilary said with a raised glass, standing next to Levi.

"Honey, you don't want to wait for your uncle?" Hilary's mom suggested.

Then Hilary blinked and looked around for her uncle.

"He probably left to go home. Just like him to come and get everyone riled up. Let's finish so I can wake up and marry my fiancé tomorrow," Hilary jested, pressing a kiss on Levi's lips.

Andi glanced around the table and stood slightly from her seat, wondering where Senator Hawthorn had gone. Then she remembered the noise from the bathroom.

"To the happy couple!" a guest shouted.

Everyone clapped, and Hilary's engagement ring flashed as she held Levi's hand.

* * *

Everything ran smoothly. Andi waited and watched as the final touches were made to Hilary's makeup. Bells rang to announce the arrival of more guests, who were asked to donate to charity instead of bringing gifts.

There was a knock on the door.

"Come in!" Hilary called, gazing into the mirror through her veil.

Her father stood outside the door. "Everyone is prepared."

Hilary said a silent prayer and checked her appearance in the mirror one last time. "I'm ready."

"You look beautiful, honey." Her dad helped her with her train and linked their arms.

Hilary waved her hand in Andi's face. "Andi."

"Huh?"

"Are you zoning out on me already?" Hilary laughed.

"No, just thinking how gorgeous you look." Andi touched her arm.

Hilary blew out a nervous breath. "Come on. We have a wedding to attend."

Hilary emerged from the dressing room with her bridal party and made her way to the entrance of the chapel.

"Now or never, Hilary," her dad whispered.

"Daddy, don't start. I'll always be your little girl." Hilary wiped the tears from his eyes.

The music started, and the doors opened to reveal the church decorated in white and silver. All the guests stood and gasped in awe. Hilary smiled and watched the bridesmaids move slowly down the aisle in front of her. She took a step when the church doors burst open on all sides, and the FBI and local police swarmed the place with their guns drawn.

"Oh, my God!" Hilary's bouquet dropped to the ground as she raised her hands in the air.

"What's the meaning of this?" Marlin shouted.

Levi rushed to Hilary and took her hand when the police interrupted.

"Everyone, stay where you are," an agent commanded.

Andi lifted her dress and marched down the aisle, shocked by the familiar gear. DC was known for its theatrics, but this was beyond the average interruption. "Victor, what's going on?" Andi demanded, resting a hand on her hip. She felt a knot of nerves in the pit of her stomach.

Victor's eyes remained glued on Andi's dress, and she waved her hand in front of his face for him to focus.

"Sorry to cut your friends' event short, but we have a situation," he said.

Her spine stiffened as he spoke. "What situation?"

"The senator is missing," Victor answered.

The congregation erupted in gasps.

"Wait, what senator?" Andi's palms became clammy.

"Senator Hawthorn."

"My uncle!" Hilary screeched.

She yanked out of Levi's hold and stomped over to Victor and Andi. Marlin and Dee hugged each other tightly.

Victor nodded, not taking his eyes off Andi. They'd been partnered up since she joined the unit seven months ago. At first, he didn't want to be associated with her because he knew it would draw heat from his coworkers. To them, Andi was a beautiful woman who shouldn't be in this line of work, and he thought people wouldn't take her seriously.

"How do you know he's missing?" Andi probed.

"We got a call and a ransom note. They won't return him unless they receive a certain amount of money," Victor explained.

"He was with us last night. I'm sure he's here." Hilary motioned around the church.

Andi scanned the guests.

"That's one of the reasons we came. I need my team to question the guests," Victor said.

"But that will take forever, and it's my wedding day!" Hilary pouted and started to cry.

Levi gripped her shoulders, turning her around to

face him. "Honey, stop crying," he said, wiping her tears away.

Victor shook his head. "Sorry, but we have a United States senator missing. This is a priority-level situation."

The police motioned for a line to be formed. Victor gestured for Andi to talk to her friend's family.

"Hilary, calm down." Andi tried to reassure her, rubbing her back.

Victor looked away while Andi pulled Hilary and Levi to the side of the church.

"Andi, do something," Hilary pleaded.

"I'm so sorry, but if he is missing, they need to investigate. I can't go against my team. What about rescheduling until tomorrow?" Andi handed over the tissues she had with her.

"You have to be kidding!" Hilary snatched the tissues out of Andi's hand.

Andi observed the FBI and police, listening to their conversations. "If it were up to me, this wouldn't be happening, Hilary, but I'm still new on the Terrorist Threat Team."

"He's probably just running late," Levi remarked.

Andi agreed with a nod to ease the tension.

"Probably. Levi, can you write down the list of guests at the dinner party last night."

Levi tapped his pockets for a pen. "You think that will help?"

"Anything to move this faster would help," Andi said.

"My uncle cannot be missing. He's a senator, for God's sake. Don't they have security?" Hilary yanked her veil off and stomped her feet.

"Baby," Levi tried to comfort her.

"Levi, make them leave," Hilary pleaded and gripped his suit jacket tightly.

"Hilary, I promise, I'll get your wedding back on track," Andi said.

Hilary shouted as she pointed at the door. "Then tell them to leave!"

Andi sighed and strolled over to Victor, who was talking to a detective.

"Sorry about this, Andi," James, the other TAT agent, spoke.

"Thanks, James. What do you know so far?" Andi asked.

"We have video footage from the restaurant, plus the note—" James began.

"I'm sorry, Andi, you're too close to this. We can't give you any information," Victor said.

Andi's dark eyes settled on him. "You're kidding me, right?"

Victor knew Andi could go on until the sun came up if someone said no to her. Surely, he didn't want to fight in front of the entire crowd of guests. "This is your best friend's wedding," he reminded her.

James watched them go back and forth.

"Don't keep me out of this. As you say, this is my best friend's wedding. I talked to the senator last night," Andi revealed.

James interrupted, "How was he?"

"He was fine and went to take a call."

"And?" Victor took notes as she talked.

"I don't know. I went to the bathroom." Andi closed her eyes when she remembered the suspicious noise from the hallway.

Victor's eyes narrowed on her. "What is it?"

Andi rubbed her forehead. "Shit," she murmured.

"You know something?" James asked.

"It could be anything." Andi had worked her whole life to get into this position and help prevent such crimes from occurring. It caused her chest to tighten. She was finding her footing in her new role, and something unexpected had happened under her watch. If word spread that the senator had been kidnapped under her nose, everyone at work would talk about her. Being the daughter of a cop brought pressure.

"Tell us." Victor crossed his arms, waiting for her to speak.

"Um, well, I heard a weird noise in the hallway after using the bathroom," Andi recalled.

"A weird noise?" he repeated.

Her eyes were puzzled. "Yeah, it was brief and not loud, but I could have sworn it was someone hurt."

"Then what happened?" Victor demanded.

"Nothing. It fell silent, and I opened the door to an empty hallway."

James and Victor regarded each other intently.

"What? You think it has something to do with the senator?" Andi probed, glancing from Victor to James.

"We need to see the footage." Victor reached into his pocket, pulled out his cell, and dialed his boss before stepping away for privacy.

Andi watched as Victor talked on the phone. "James, tell me the truth."

"I agree that it could be nothing, but I'm of the firm belief that anything can turn into something," James said, checking his earpiece.

Andi lingered, waiting for Victor to finish, when Hilary's parents approached.

"Andi, tell us the truth. Is my brother missing?" Marlin Hawthorn asked.

Andi felt the weight of the world on her shoulders. Bad news on a day like today would only cause grief. "Mr. and Mrs. Hawthorn—"

"Andi, we need you to come with us," Victor interrupted before she spoke further.

Marlin frowned. "Wait, Victor."

"Mr. Hawthorn. I'm sorry, but we can't answer any more questions for you at the moment. Once we have more information, I'll update you." Victor wrapped his hand around Andi's elbow and escorted her outside.

She knew what he was doing but felt they should know the truth. "What was that about?" Andi snatched out of his hold, heart pounding rapidly.

"You can't give details on an open case."

She pointed at the church. "I wasn't giving out details, and besides, they're family to me."

"Doesn't matter. You need to change, and we need to get back so I can check the footage." Victor walked off to get in the G-ride.

Andi stood at the top of the stairs.

Victor stood with the door open. "What are you waiting on?"

"I don't have any clothes here," Andi muttered in exasperation.

"Fine, I'll drive you home." Andi stomped down the stairs with her dress in hand and climbed in the passenger door.

Victor quipped, "You look nice."

"Thanks," she muttered as he entered the traffic before speeding back home.

Whether her boss would let her work the case was

unclear. His reaction would be different if he found out she'd leaked any information before it became public. She could kiss her career goodbye.

Andi remembered she hadn't seen Whitney arrive at the church and took out her phone.

Andi: *Hey. Are you on your way to the church?*

Whitney: *No, I got caught up in traffic.*

She felt a little relief.

Andi: *An emergency came up. Can't talk now. Call Hilary.*

Whitney: *Is everything all right?*

Andi: *Fine, but go home and I'll call you later.*

Victor looked at Andi. "I hope you know I didn't want to barge in like that."

"Matter of perspective."

Thirty minutes later, they arrived at her apartment. After parking, Victor removed the key, and they left the car, heading toward the front entrance of her building in silence.

Chapter Two

Before discovering Andi was an agent, most people thought she was a high fashion model because of her tall, athletic build. She had a small button nose, high cheekbones, and long, honey-blonde hair, which gave the impression of a girly girl.

But Andi Easton would prove many people wrong when it came to processing a crime scene or questioning a suspect. They tried many times to get under her skin. At times she played to her advantage, especially in training, because the men thought she'd be down in the first round. Most of the time, it was they who gave up when she twisted an arm or punched someone in the stomach.

Andi came out of her room and lifted her vest, grabbing her badge, keys, and purse. "Ready," she said, entering the living room.

Victor stood in the middle of the apartment with his phone to his ear. He stared at the transformation from a dressed-up Andi to a business Andi. "Let me call you back." He ended the call.

Andi reached for the door. "Did the footage get to the

office?" Andi let Victor walk out first, then locked the door behind herself.

Victor answered, "It's there."

"I hope he's fine and this was all a mistake."

"Based on the note, I think we have a problem." Victor pushed the elevator button.

Before the door closed, a hand cut in to block it from closing, and a few college girls stepped on, whispering to each other.

"Do you have it on you?" Andi questioned.

"Back at the office." Victor smiled at the two girls who waved at him.

The doors opened to the main lobby. They let the girls off first, then proceeded to the exit doors. One girl turned to wave at him, and he smirked. Andi wanted to wring his neck but ignored the flirting. She'd clashed with Victor from the beginning, but lately, he'd been better, and they'd started to form a great working relationship.

There was a chance Senator Hawthorn was drunk in bed with one of the many women he kept on the side. It was a secret only a few people knew. Andi learned from growing up with Hilary when she visited and listened to Dee talk with friends about her brother-in-law's cheating.

Andi grabbed her ringing phone out of her purse and saw Hilary's name across. She showed Victor. "It's Hilary."

"Answer it."

She wrinkled her nose at him. "What should I tell her?"

"Nothing."

Her lips fell apart. "Victor."

. . .

In the car, Victor hit the turn signal and slid into the far-left lane to drive back to the office. "Andi, you know as well as I that everyone is a suspect until we can pinpoint."

The phone stopped ringing, and she blew out a breath. The Terrorist Threat Assessment Team was created for domestic and foreign situations precisely like this. Since growing up in a police and military family, it was known that she would go down a path of service. Being single with no kids allowed her to accept her position and travel. Her skills in the field captured the notice of the higher-ups, who eventually offered her the Terrorist Threat Assessment Team position, which prevented attacks on US soil.

"I hear you. I feel bad it all happened at her wedding."

Victor pushed her into agent mode. "How was Ted acting last night?"

"Same as usual. He was late and flirty with the women."

Victor had heard all the rumors about Ted too. "He's known in DC as a big flirt."

"Yeah. Growing up, I spent time at Hilary's house, and Uncle Ted visited along with his wife."

"You call him Uncle Ted?" Victor pressed.

"No. He said to call him that, but I ignored it and went by Mr. Hawthorn."

Ten minutes later, Victor arrived at headquarters and showed his badge. The gate opened, and he drove toward the employee's entrance and his reserved spot.

"Only a matter of time before it hits the press." Victor shut the door.

Andi came around, sliding her badge over her neck. "How much in ransom?"

"Not a lot, and that seems weird."

"You think something else is behind the money?"

"What do all terrorists want?" Victor looked at Andi.

"Attention that brings death and destruction," Andi answered.

He nodded as they went through the security post and into the elevator.

The doors opened, and Andi stepped off into a room in a frenzy as phones rang off the hook, and the TV replayed the video of the Terrorist Threat Assessment Team busting up the wedding.

"How did they get this footage?" Victor pointed at the screen.

"That's why Hilary was calling me." Andi dropped her purse and keys on the table.

"We have unconfirmed breaking news. Hilary Hawthorn and Levi Baldwin's wedding was interrupted by an FBI terrorist unit and local law enforcement," the news anchor spoke.

Assistant Deputy Director William Morgan yelled, "Agent Easton!"

"Shit," Victor cursed under his breath when their boss stomped over to them.

"My office. Now!" Director Morgan yelled.

Victor and Andi treaded to his office.

"Sir—" Andi was halted by his hand in the air to stop talking.

"Close the door," Director Morgan said.

"Yes, sir," Andi replied, fidgeting with her hands.

They took a seat and waited for him to speak. "What is this I hear about you being involved in releasing information?" Director Morgan narrowed his eyes at Andi.

"I didn't."

"Agent Easton, you've been with us for seven months. I don't want any whining. Do you have any idea how much I put on the line with the higher-ups not to have you thrown out of here?" he shouted, slamming his hand on the desk.

"Sir, I assure you I haven't given out any information."

"So why are reporters stuffing their noses around my case at the restaurant?" His tone was harsh.

"It wasn't me, sir."

"I believe her, sir. As soon as I got to the church, she was with me all afternoon," Victor explained.

Andi prayed it would help her case.

Morgan tapped his pen on the desk and glared at Andi. Women had it extra hard in the unit, and Director Morgan understood how difficult it could be to win acceptance, but he never gave out favoritism to anyone.

He relaxed, leaning back in his chair. "Where are we with everything?" Morgan questioned.

"The interviews should come in soon, but I need to watch the footage from the restaurant," Victor explained.

"Fine. Get through that and send a notice to all the local news stations. This is an ongoing case, and nothing is to be discussed," Director Morgan instructed.

Andi waited for the hammer to drop.

"Understood." Victor stood and turned to leave, and Andi followed when Morgan called her name.

"Agent Easton, I should remove you from this case, but I won't. Make sure I don't regret it," Director Morgan stated.

"Thank you, Director Morgan." Andi released a breath of relief and marched to her desk.

Victor sat across from her and logged into his

computer. Andi checked her email before pulling the contact for Senator Hawthorn's office on her phone.

"Andi, check this out." Victor motioned for her to come to his desk.

Andi dropped the phone and walked around to his desk. Victor replayed the video. It started with her getting up from the table after the senator took the call and heading to the bathroom. Then skips to Hilary, holding up a glass of champagne, about to give a speech.

"That can't be it."

"Someone didn't want us to see what happened."

Andi's office phone rang.

"Answer it. I'll keep running this clip. If it's Hilary, tell her we're still working the case," Victor said.

Andi lifted the phone. "Agent Easton."

"Andi Easton of Terrorist Assessment?" The gravely robotic voice asked.

Andi's brows squinted in confusion. "This is her." She removed the phone from her ear and placed the call on speaker.

The voice chuckled. "Agent, I've heard wonderful things about you."

"Who is this?" Andi reached into her pocket to grab a pen and paper.

"A friend, Agent."

Victor sat up straight in irritation.

Anxiety cooled Andi's thoughts. "What do you want?"

Victor wrote on a piece of paper, holding up the sign to another officer to trace the call.

"Actually, it should be; what do you want?"

"You have me at a disadvantage. What's your name?"

Victor motioned his hand for her to keep talking.

"That's not important right now. I know your partner is trying to trace this call."

She repeated, "I'd like to know your name."

"In due time, but the better question is, where is Senator Hawthorn?"

Andi leaned forward in her chair, and her eyes ballooned wide. "Where is he?"

He chuckled. "Safe for now, but that can change in a blink of an eye."

"Tell me what you want?"

"The Hawthorns have taken from people far too long, and it's time to pay back."

"All right, I hear you." She tried to stay calm and flailed her hand in the air, asking if they caught the trace.

"Please don't give me that psychological bullshit. This isn't my first run."

"We can figure this out together," Andi reassured him.

"Oh, we will. Just remember, I wanted to be a friend," the voice stated before the line went dead.

"Damn it! Did you get anything?" Andi looked at Jonathan, the other agent listening in on the call.

"It was too short and scrambled," Jonathan replied.

"We need to get back to the restaurant." Andi looked at Victor.

"Check the note out first," Victor reminded, pulling it out of the case file and handing it to her.

Hawthorn is sentenced to death unless you release these two men. The note went on to request a swap of two prisoners for Hawthorn. There were no negotiations with terrorists in the US, so they wouldn't release Paul Adams and Simon Denton, who were sentenced two years ago for conspiring to commit terrorist acts. Among those who voted to include a life sentence without parole in the bill was Hawthorn.

"Do you know anything about the case involving Paul and Simon?" Andi logged into her computer, navigated to the case database, and typed in their names to pull up their files. She scrolled through the information and jotted down the case file notes.

"I heard about them, but I didn't pay much attention," Victor recalled.

Andi shook her head. "This is personal."

"The longer he's missing, the more difficult it will get."

"Should we try his home first or the restaurant?"

Victor checked his watch. "Depending on the phone call, we don't have much time."

"Should we split up?" She passed the paper to Jonathan.

"We should go to the restaurant, then to his home."

"Jonathan, get those files brought up ASAP and start reading every detail to see if they had any help," Andi commanded.

Jonathan nodded and headed to the file room. Victor slipped the note into the evidence bag, and Andi logged off and grabbed her things.

"I hope we find him soon," Andi muttered to herself once in the elevator.

* * *

Hilary called again, but Andi avoided her calls. They were becoming more frequent throughout the day. The whole situation still confused Andi, and she wasn't ready to speak with Hilary, who needed answers. The hostess allowed them to proceed without a reservation after she pointed at the bartender. As soon as Andi showed her badge, the bartender finished pouring wine for a couple.

"Hey, I remember you." He grinned and lifted a napkin on the counter.

"Good, because I need help." Andi smiled.

"Sure thing, sexy."

Andi showed her badge. "Agent Easton."

His grin disappeared. "How can I help you?"

"Your name?" Victor questioned.

"Um, Terry."

Andi slipped her business card on the bar top. "I was here last night with friends, and I want to know if you closed up last night."

"I did. I close everything at night."

"Did you see or hear anything strange?"

"No, I mean... the regular drunk people." He shrugged, picking up her business card.

Victor stood behind her and watched the bartender for any weird movements. Their training had prepared them to watch for any signs of deceit or hesitation.

"Senator Hawthorn took a call, right?"

Terry placed two glasses on the bar and refilled the dish tray with dirty glasses. "Yeah, it didn't last long."

"Do you remember who he talked to?"

"No, I was kind of busy working the bar. We had someone out sick last night."

As a potential lead, Andi thought it was worth following up. "Who called out sick?"

"Why? Sarah wouldn't be mixed up in anything like that."

"Sarah's a bartender?" Andi probed, happy he was talking.

"A waitress, but sometimes she helps with the bar," he responded.

"Is the owner here?"

"No, he's only here twice a week. Jared feels it's beneath him to show up when he has a manager." Terry laughed.

"Give me the names." Andi handed him a pen and a napkin to write them down.

Victor scanned the area in the hallway and walked up to the camera facing the front entrance.

The door to the bathroom opened, and a waitress wiped her hands before tossing the towel in the trash. "You can forget that camera. It's been broken for a while."

"How long have you worked here?" Victor asked, pushing the men's' bathroom door open.

"About five years. Why?"

"What's your name?"

"Am I in trouble?" She crossed her hands over her chest, her face forming a frown.

Andi watched the nervousness appear. "Should you be in trouble?"

"No, I mean... besides a few parking tickets." She gulped.

"Name?" Victor's brow hiked up.

She whispered, "Melissa."

"Melissa, I'm Victor. Did you work last night?" He removed his wallet and pulled out a business card.

"I was off."

"Well, if you can think of anything or spoke with anyone that worked last night, I'd appreciate your help." Victor gave her a wink; she smiled and almost bumped into Andi.

"Excuse me," Melissa said, shifting around her.

"What did he say?"

"Not much, but I have the information for the owner and manager," Andi replied.

"Turn that up!" a voice called.

They ran from around the corner to look at the big screen behind the bar with breaking news of a building reduced to rubble. Fire and smoke erupted as the fire department worked to put it out, and ambulances covered the street.

"First warning," Andi murmured.

Victor glanced at her. "You think it's them?"

The moment he tried to antagonize her, wanting to be a friend, she knew he would strike first.

"We need to get over there." Andi turned to leave.

Victor watched as a few people were led out of their homes. So far, no casualties had been reported, and Andi figured it was likely a warning shot.

Andi exited the restaurant and looked back at the bathroom, trying to recall anything from the night before.

"The guy from the bathroom," she muttered.

"What did you say?"

"There was a guy who came out of the men's' bathroom."

"Why didn't you say something sooner?" Victor looked at her and hopped into his designated vehicle.

"Because I didn't know what happened, and he said he didn't hear anything." She secured her seat belt while Victor turned on the ignition.

"Remember, anything can be a clue." Victor put the car in drive and fastened his seat belt. He pressed the gas and handed her his phone.

"What am I doing with this?"

"Look through the photos and pick out the man you saw. We can get the guys to run a trace."

They were about ten minutes from the site of the explosion, so Andi scrolled through each face as they headed there.

"Anything?" Victor asked.

"Not yet."

Passing through the light, Victor continued driving down the street. "Keep looking."

While contemplating whether going on the case would result in more deaths, Andi missed calls from her family and friends.

Chapter Three

Victor arrived, found a parking space not too far from an ambulance, and jumped out, shaking hands with a few local officers. Andi looked at the crowd around the area held back behind yellow lines by the police. Her gut told her someone was watching, and after the phone call she'd received at the office, it made sense to think it was all connected.

Andi went over to stand next to Victor as the fire department finished getting the place under order.

"What can you tell us?" Victor questioned the officer on duty.

"All I know is that we got a call to come here."

"Got a call?"

The officer nodded. "Yeah, we were at the station, and the call came through that there would be an explosion."

Andi asked, "So they gave you a warning?"

"Strange, I know, but we decided to come."

"Anyone hurt?"

"No, but this area isn't known for having the best reputation," the officer answered.

"Thank you, Officer Elliot," Andi replied, looking at his name tag.

Victor watched her head toward the building, ignoring the calls from the police officers.

"What time did you get the call?" Andi yelled back.

"Honestly don't remember. Maybe an hour ago," Officer Elliot responded, following behind her.

"An hour ago I was still at the wedding," Andi recalled.

"Wedding?" Officer Elliot muttered.

"That's enough time if they already had the bomb here and if they're watching you."

"We need to look at all the people who dealt with the bill signing," Andi announced.

"Either it's all connected through you or the senator's disappearance."

"Shit, let me take this," Andi murmured as her phone rang, moving away from Victor and

Officer Elliot.

"Andi!" Hillary cried into the phone.

"Hilary, calm down."

"You have to get here now!"

Andi paced and covered her ear to try and hear Hilary. "Where are you?"

"Levi and I went to my parent's home, and we got a video."

"I'll be right there."

"Please, Andi. They're talking about Levi having something to do with the

disappearance."

"Don't worry, Hilary. I'm on my way."

Things weren't adding up for Andi, and she needed to get to the bottom of who was behind all these problems. As soon as she started out of the building with Victor behind her, gunshots rang out.

"Get down!" Andi shouted, dropping to the ground as the crowd scrambled to find shelter.

Victor pulled out his gun in disbelief at police officers being shot at in broad daylight.

Everything moved in slow motion, and Andi clambered close to him and back into the building to regroup. "What's going on?"

"We need backup."

"Had to be the plan all along," Andi said breathlessly.

"What?" Officer Elliot asked.

"To get us here and out in the open," Andi responded. She raised her gun and returned fire.

"We have at least five officers and three civilians dead," Victor announced and started to shoot again.

More police sirens joined the chaos, and Andi listened for more shots. Nothing went off, so she stood and slowly started out of the building.

"Andi! Get back here."

"Either they'll make a move, or I'll die. I'm not staying here forever."

Gunfire erupted again.

Andi saw a tall guy with dirty blond hair and a lanky build shoot at her from the side of a blue van. She started to fire back and then chased after him as the van started and drove away.

Andi cursed, out of breath from running, "Fuck!"

"Are you crazy?" Victor yelled.

"Not now, Victor."

"You got a death wish?"

"We can't be sitting ducks forever."

* * *

Hilary and Levi sat on the couch when Andi appeared at her cousin's home later that afternoon. She hugged her aunt and uncle. Victor went back to the office to go over the day's shooting, and Andi confirmed she'd be in early the next day after talking things over with her family.

Hilary jumped up and hugged Andi. "So glad you're here."

"Tell me what's going on."

"After you left with the FBI, we got this video." Hilary picked up the remote and pointed it at the TV screen.

"Is that...?"

"Yeah, my uncle. I can't believe he looks so disheveled. He probably thinks we've forgotten about him." She hugged herself.

"Where did it come from?"

It seemed they'd kept the Senator alive, possibly for ransom. He was in the same clothes from the event, but his eyes were drooping, and he had the beginnings of a beard around his chin. They'd placed him in front of a camera with a newspaper of the current date.

"It was here when we got home."

"Do you still have cameras on the property?"

"We already checked the cameras, and it was delivered by somebody in a white delivery van," her aunt recalled.

"I need to take the tape with me," Andi explained.

Hilary scanned Andi. "Do you think he's dead?"

Andi grabbed Hilary's hand and squeezed as Levi

circled his arm around her shoulders. Her parents stood behind her, also embracing.

Andi rose off the couch and reached into her pocket as her phone rang. Levi removed the tape, and regular TV aired again, depicting a breaking story of the shoot-out from earlier.

"Andi, you're on TV." Hilary pointed at the screen, and Andi listened to Victor on the phone while the shoot-out scene played out.

"You need to come into the office," Victor stated.

Andi zeroed in on the screen of herself in pursuit of the van that drove away from the scene. "My friend needs me," she replied through stiff lips.

"The boss is pissed and wants to talk to you."

She sighed, running a hand down her face. "Fine."

She knew complications would arise from her decision to go after the shooter. Andi slid the phone into her pocket, turned to her family, and told them she needed to head back to the office.

"Will you keep us updated if you find him?" Dee prodded for answers.

Andi answered, "You'll be the first to know."

After reassuring her family she'd do everything to get the people behind the kidnapping, Andi started back on the road toward her building, keeping the radio off while lost in thought.

Fifteen minutes later, she arrived and stepped out of the elevator to chaos in the FBI office. A cacophony of phones rang nonstop, and coworkers yelled back and forth. Victor gestured for her just as their boss blocked her movements.

Director Morgan's familiar mask descended once again. "My office. Now."

Andi dropped her head and strolled to his office.

He left the door open and paced in front of his desk as she came in behind him, pulling it closed.

Morgan hiked his brow. "Do you like your job?"

Andi stammered, "Yes, sir."

"Something deep down tells me to fire you." He held a resigned posture.

"Director Morgan—"

"No, you listen. I have every news station in the state calling me."

She paused. "I—"

"Quiet. You're too close to this case and doing your own thing."

"But, sir, I have—"

He raised a hand to cut her off. "If I hear of you doing anything else like today, you can turn in your badge, Agent."

"Come in!" he yelled as someone knocked on the door. It opened to reveal Victor. "Any news on the officers that got shot?" Morgan walked around to sit at his desk.

"Two are in critical condition. The other three have minor injuries."

"I know I was wrong to make that call without talking to my partner," Andi said.

"Glad you know that."

Andi removed the tape from her pocket. "Hilary's parents had a visitor today."

Victor took the tape, pushed it into the recorder, and hit play.

"That's the senator," her boss muttered.

Andi nodded. "While we were at the explosion, they sent this video."

The senator looked despondent, and his hands shook

as he held the current newspaper in front of the camera. Nothing in the background gave any clue to his location. He had a small scar across his brow from a possible blow to the face.

"Get this over to our team to run fingerprints and time stamps," their boss commanded.

Andi glanced at Victor, then her boss. "Am I allowed to stay on the case?"

"Do everything by the book, Easton."

"Yes, sir."

"Victor, put some people on her family's property and Andi's apartment."

Andi gnawed on her bottom lip. "I don't need protection."

"Either you follow my rules, or you're off the task force."

"Andi, once they made contact, you became a target."

They knew everybody was breathing down their necks to get the senator back safely, or it would be their jobs. Too much public pressure would set off more opportunities for terrorists to think it's easy to kidnap political figures.

Chapter Four

The next day, Andi turned the hot shower off and dried with the towel, rubbing through her hair. She barely got any sleep last night once she made it home and to bed because her thoughts were on yesterday's shooting.

Victor promised their boss he'd stick beside her at all times, so she knew going off on her own wouldn't work.

Andi came out of the bathroom, blow-dried her hair, and pulled it into a tight ponytail.

"Here, you look like you need this." Whitney pushed a cup of coffee into her hands.

Andi sipped. "Thanks."

"Hilary told me everything." Whitney sat on the chair in her bedroom and watched her put on minimal makeup.

"Heartbreaking."

"Have you talked to your parents?"

Andi sighed. "Not yet, but I will."

"Aaron said your mother tried to contact you." Whitney and Andi knew that was a lie.

"I'll call my father and brother to make sure they're good." Andi finished putting on her shoes.

"The hospitals are on high alert," Whitney announced. "Maybe you should take some time off work."

"I love my job. They won't run me away."

"It's not about running away."

Andi grabbed the mug of coffee and left her bedroom with Whitney on her trail.

"Hilary and Levi plan on eloping."

Andi whipped around to face her. "Her parents okay with eloping?"

A hint of hesitation crept into her eyes. "Hilary is spoiled at the end of the day," Whitney responded.

After she secured her 9mm and moisturized her hands, Andi entered the kitchen and refilled her morning coffee. Andi's eyes shot up in surprise at the knock at the door, and she looked at the clock on the wall to see it was eight-thirty in the morning. Whitney sat on the stool facing the counter as Andi stalked to the door and looked through the peephole. She saw Victor with a bag in his hand.

"I thought we were meeting at the office," she said, throwing open the door.

Victor passed Andi the bag of food, grabbed the mug of coffee out of her hand, and took a sip. "Ew, I hate cream in my coffee." His face scrunched in disgust.

"Good, because this is my coffee." Andi opened the bag and took out a breakfast wrap from the local bakery where they usually hung out.

"You haven't met Whitney before. This is my other best friend."

Victor extended a hand and told her to stay seated.

"Usually, I would, but before we head in, we need to talk."

"Victor, I don't need a babysitter."

"Yesterday proves you do."

"Look, I apologize, but my family is involved."

Whitney jumped up. "I'll call you later, Andi. Nice to meet you, Victor." Andi showed her friend to the door, and they hugged goodbye.

"And I would be as frustrated, but other people got hurt because of your actions," Victor continued once Whitney had left.

Andi was wary and anxious at the thought of not finding the senator.

"Is something more going on with you?"

"No." Andi took a seat at the kitchen island.

Those eyes she tried to avoid peered at her.

"I swear." Andi held her hands up in surrender.

Victor's broad shoulders dropped. He came to sit next to her on the stool and removed his food. "The video didn't give anything away for us to get closer to who's holding him."

"Damn."

"Yeah, I'm not happy about being in the dark."

"Whoever is behind his kidnapping has resources," Andi pointed out.

"Resources?"

"Almost too easy."

Victor frowned. "Should we go back to the restaurant?"

"I think it's a good idea to talk with the staff again, hell, even the people who signed the bill."

"We don't have enough time," Victor reminded her.

"Are you driving or me?" Andi stood from her seat.

Victor took a bite of his food and groaned. "Me. You're a terrible driver."

They came out of the building and into Victor's car, and Andi smiled at one of Victor's lame jokes as he opened the car door. Suddenly, time stood still, and Andi felt a prickle on the back of her neck.

An enormous explosion rent the air a few blocks from Andi's apartment building. The ground shook, and people screamed and ran for cover.

"Andi!" Victor yelled as horns blasted.

Screams echoed, and buses crashed into cars. Andi scanned the scene around her in utter despair. The ringing in her ear wouldn't stop, and the crowd started to push to get away from the fire and smoke.

"Help me!" a woman wept.

Andi slowly got up from the ground.

"Are you hurt?" Victor asked, lifting her chin. He rubbed dust from her face, and she waved her hand in front of her to avoid the smoke.

The same woman pleaded, "Help, please!"

"Call for backup. I got her." Victor reached into his pocket and passed her his phone.

No sooner did she take it than it rang, and Andi held it to her ear.

"Agent Easton. We should be closer by now," the familiar voice came on the line.

"Tell me your name right now."

"Did you like my new surprise?"

She hissed, "Listen to me very carefully."

He scoffed. "No, you listen. I run you now."

"Tell me what you want, or I'm hanging up."

"Simple, to release them and the money."

"Money we can talk, but releasing convicts will never happen."

He chortled. "More fun surprises will happen."

Fire trucks, ambulances, and the police arrived as Andi watched in horror at the drama unfolding. The same blue van from the first explosion pulled off at the corner.

"Gotcha." Andi dropped the call and bolted down the street as Victor helped a few people get support from EMTs.

"Andi!" Victor shouted, running after her as she pushed through the streets between people, broken glass, and vehicle pileups.

Andi came around the corner with her gun drawn to an empty alleyway.

"Andi!" An out-of-breath Victor removed his gun and took the safety off.

"I got another call." Andi dropped her hands and planted them on her hips to catch her breath.

"What did they say?"

"To release those two men."

"Maybe we can trace the call again."

"Doubt it. Seems to be ahead of us at every turn."

Andi knew she needed to get a handle on the phone calls and take control, or the entire city would be destroyed unless two terrorists were set free.

"I need to go over the files again."

"Let's go." Victor and Andi walked out of the alley and sprinted back to the vehicle.

* * *

Andi slammed the files on the table, picked up the coke, and took a sip. She flipped over the photos from the first incident reported at the restaurant. Victor wrote a time-line on the whiteboard from the moment the senator went missing. The agency sent over everything on the bills, and the senators signed off and watched the testimony.

"Something seems off."

Victor turned to look at her. "Off like the timing of the bombs?"

Andi closed her eyes and drowned out his words. She tried to draw on her training, but everything she'd been taught to be ready for had come into play all at once. "Feels like we're being used."

"Keep talking." Victor dropped the marker on the table and hovered.

She showed no signs of relenting. "They don't care about killing people, and it escalated fairly quickly."

"Yeah."

Noise rumbled all around them. "Why this senator out of everyone who participated in the bill's creation?"

Victor shrugged his shoulders and slipped his hands into his pockets. "To get their friends
out of jail."

"No, it's more than that." Andi stood and walked to the whiteboard, picking up another marker. "Hilary is marrying Levi, a man from a family with money. Well, eloping, probably."

"Eloping? Okay."

Andi picked up the file, saw the number of names, and counted in her head. "Each senator on the bill comes from money."

"Possibly personal."

"We've gone around in circles, and they've made it a

point to hurt people if we don't release some terrorists. Nothing else was stated."

"Keep going."

Andi highlighted the senator's name. "No other connection beyond a bill that comes and goes in congress. We've seen it many times."

"Senator has enemies, Andi."

"Not to the extent of bombs going off in the city."

The door opened, and Director Morgan entered, looking grim. "They found a body near the church where the wedding was held."

A lump formed in her throat. "Have they identified the body?"

"Not yet. I want you out there now. Press is going crazy for updates."

"If it's the senator, the president is going to have to make a statement," Andi pointed out.

Her boss aimed a finger at her. "I want answers, and now, Agent."

Late afternoon came, and Andi listened to her father talk in her ear about what she should be doing and how to handle the various updates.

"Dad, I just got home and haven't had a second to eat." Andi held onto the bag of groceries and slid the key in the lock when she noticed a piece of paper stuck on the door.

"The body they found could have been Ted's. You got lucky."

Andi opened the note.

Third time's a charm.

Ignoring her father, Andi swiftly dropped the bag. She pulled out her gun, jogged down the hall to the exit doors, and scanned the area. She returned as her neighbor's door opened, and Andi startled her with her gun in her face.

"Oh, my God!" her elderly neighbor screamed.

"Sorry, Gretchen. Stay in your apartment."

"Is something wrong, Andi?" Gretchen questioned. The entire building knew she was the biggest gossiper and in everyone's business.

"Everything is fine." Andi pushed her door open with her gun ready and slowly eased down the hallway, not paying attention to Gretchen behind her until she tripped over her shoe.

Gretchen drew in her breath sharply.

"Gretchen, you scared me."

"Sorry, you seemed on the go and looked like you needed backup." Gretchen held her baseball bat in her hand.

Andi picked up her phone and saw her father calling back. "I promise it's fine... Hello, Dad." Andi walked Gretchen out and shut the door.

"You hung up on me," Dad grumbled.

"Sorry, I needed to check out something."

"Are you in trouble?"

Andi lifted the note to read again. "Someone is going to be."

Chapter Five

Victor listened to Andi explain and wasted no time getting the security footage from the building. The screen showed the security guard allowing a few people up and one delivery person with flowers who dropped them off in the trash before taping the note to her door.

"Did any of your neighbors see anything?"

"No, and Gretchen would know."

"This is becoming personal. Where was your detail?"

"I sent them home because I didn't need to be crowded."

"Director wants to pull you off the case," Victor muttered.

Andi scowled. "It makes sense to use me because they choose to communicate with only me."

"That's the problem. We have to pinpoint the call traces."

"I need to talk to Hilary and Levi again."

"I'll go with you."

As Andi and Victor stepped out of the conference room, their tech, Peter, approached.

"Andi, I think I got a hit." Peter held a folder in his hand.

"Show me," Andi answered.

Peter sat at his cubicle, removed the photos, and pointed at the blue van she'd been seeing at every turn.

"DC Flower Galore," Andi read the name of the business and glanced at the picture of the man from her apartment, who appeared to be driving the van.

"The same guy," Peter said.

"Who is he?"

"He tried to hide his face as much as possible, but the camera from the church and your building matched him in height and facial recognition, Leslie Witherberg," Peter explained.

"A criminal record?" Victor wondered.

"A long rap sheet of robberies and disorderly conduct," Peter stated.

"How does it connect to the senator?"

"That's what we're trying to figure out."

"Can I take these with me?" Andi asked.

"Sure, and sorry about your friend's family."

"Thanks, Peter."

Victor and Andi shook hands with Peter and left the office on a mission. Andi drove with a lot on her mind, listening to the directions for the DC flower shop while Victor typed on his phone.

"Take a look at this interesting detail." Victor held the phone up with a photo of the flower shop's delivery van matching the van Leslie drove.

"My gut is telling me it's more than Leslie setting the bombs off."

"I agree, but we need to find him first."

Shortly after, Andi pulled up to a closed, abandoned building with a DC Flower Galore sign half gone. She found a space, and they hopped out, walked up to the front door, and peered through the dusty windows.

Victor tried to open the door. "Bet the building is used as a front."

"My father always said if you feel like you're spinning your wheels, it means you need to reshuffle the deck," Andi announced.

"I think your pops is right."

"All I know is that one more bomb is going off, and we need to find it first."

"Start at the source."

Andi looked at Victor. "Hawthorns."

* * *

Andi raised her hand to knock on Marlin's front door when it was snatched open, and the house manager stepped to the side, allowing them entry.

"Hilary, is Levi here?" Andi asked, entering the kitchen.

"He's at work."

"Who else is here with you?"

"My dad. Why?"

"We need to talk to you both."

"Any news on my uncle?"

"That's what we need to talk about."

Hilary strolled out of the kitchen and found her father in his office on the telephone.

"I'll call you back." He hung up and started to stand.

Andi held her hand up. "Mr. Hawthorn, please stay seated."

"Do you have news on Ted?" Marlin asked.

Andi clasped her hands together. "Do you know Leslie Witherberg?"

Victor stood off in the corner and watched Marlin's demeanor.

"No, should I?"

"Have you ever ordered flowers from DC Flower Galore?" Andi looked for facial tics or signs of him lying.

"Andi, what's with all the questions for my father? I know he's not a suspect." Hilary chuckled, but no one else was laughing.

"We have no leads, but two bombs have gone off with dozens injured or dead. The only lead we have is Leslie Witherberg."

"I've ordered flowers for my wife plenty of times. I don't remember where," Marlin answered.

Andi pressed, "Think hard, please."

"Sorry, Andi. I can't help you."

"Levi has ordered flowers for me before," Hilary remarked.

"From this place?" Andi held up the logo of the company."

"A few times." Hilary shrugged.

Andi and Victor glanced at each other.

"Where did you say Levi was?"

"At work, but what does this have to do with my uncle?" Hilary crossed her arms over her chest.

Victor stepped further into the room. "Did Levi and your uncle have a business relationship at any point?"

Hilary gazed at him, then Andi. "Andi, are you

accusing Levi of being behind my uncle's disappearance?"

"Hilary, think hard. Have Levi and Ted worked on some business dealings?"

"Andi, I think that's enough questions for Hilary," Marlin commanded.

"Actually, we're only getting started," Victor defended.

There was laughter outside the door, and then Hilary's mom appeared. "Andi! I didn't expect you here so soon. Any news on Ted?" Dee inquired.

Andi shook her head. "No updates, Dee."

"Andi and her partner are on their way out," Hilary stated.

Andi wanted to be more forceful but felt sorry for putting her best friend through questioning like a criminal, so she left it alone.

The door shut behind them, and Andi released an aggravated grunt of annoyance.

"You know she's going to call and warn him now."

"I expected nothing else." Andi sighed and glanced at Victor.

"Can you see yourself arresting him if he's guilty?" Victor challenged.

Andi stared forward in deep thought at all the memories of Hilary, Levi, and her together.

"Honestly, I can't answer that right now."

Victor pressed the gas and exited the driveway to the next destination.

Director Morgan wanted answers as soon as possible before the next bomb went off. Andi worried that things could have turned out differently if she'd paid more attention the night of the engagement party.

* * *

"Let me do the talking," Andi insisted as she and Victor arrived at Levi's reception desk.

Victor smirked. "I know you're close to him, so you can lead for now."

Andi glanced at Victor and gathered he'd be trouble if she didn't control the conversation with Levi.

The secretary finished her call and smiled at them. "Hello, welcome to Baldwin Inc. How may I help you?"

"Is Levi here?"

"May I ask what this is regarding?"

"I'm a close friend of Hilary and Levi."

"Name?"

"Andi Easton."

She lifted the phone and dialed his line for confirmation.

Andi tapped her foot while she waited and looked around his office. As a lobbyist, Levi was into all the political wrangling that DC loved to trash on TV. But behind the scenes, money talked.

"He's available. You can go right in now." The secretary motioned to the door, and they

thanked her.

Andi slipped her hand around the knob and tapped on the door, poking her head in.

Levi grinned and jumped up, walking around his desk with his arms stretched out for a hug. "Andi! Never seen you at my office before. Nice surprise."

Levi stepped back and extended a hand to Victor. "You remember Agent Conway."

"Yes, from the church."

"Mr. Baldwin," Victor responded.

Levi gestured to take a seat. "Hilary called and said you'd be on your way."

"I won't hold you up too long, Levi. We have a few questions."

"About Ted Hawthorn?"

Andi glanced at Victor. "Leslie Witherberg."

"Not familiar with the name."

Andi slipped her hand into her pocket and removed the photo of the DC flower shop. "Do you recognize this man or the flower shop?"

Levi rubbed his chin and stared at the photo. "Sorry. I have my assistant order flowers for

Hilary all the time, so I never pay attention." He gave the photo back.

"You like your job, Levi?"

He chuckled. "Who doesn't?"

"The kidnapping of Ted Hawthorn is connected to Leslie and the bombs going off around

the city."

Levi's face grew red. "Are you saying you think I have something to do with this person?"

"At the moment, you're the best lead we have."

Levi argued, "As my best friend, I thought you'd have more faith in me."

"Then tell us if your company had anything to do with the bill that Ted Hawthorn voted on," Victor challenged.

Levi sighed in exasperation and sat back in deep thought.

"All right."

"All right, what?"

"We invested in making sure the bill wouldn't push through."

Andi's heart sank. "Levi, they're criminals."

"Hear me out, Andi."

Andi jumped up in anger. "Are you telling me you're behind not wanting a terrorist bill passed into law that would help take them off the streets?"

"That bill was full of stuff that had nothing to do with keeping criminals out of jail," Levi argued.

"So you've become one of them."

"I'm still Levi from college. Your best friend."

"I'm not sure who you are. Hilary know about any of the work you do?"

"No."

"Great."

"She knows my family is in politics, but not the extent."

"My God, Levi."

"Everything we do is legal."

"Doesn't make it right!" Andi shouted.

"Andi, he's right," Victor commented, and Andi whirled to face them.

"Whoever took Ted has nothing to do with me or my company."

"You better pray that's true." Andi stormed out of his office.

Victor jogged to catch up as Andi pressed the elevator button repeatedly. "Are you willing to do what needs to be done?" Victor let Andi step on the elevator first and watched Levi on the phone as the doors closed.

"I'm an agent first, Victor."

"Then we get a tail on him now and trace his calls."

The elevator doors opened, and they headed back to the car. Andi passed Victor the keys, and he opened the door. She slammed the door and released a breath.

Victor weaved in and out of traffic to give her a moment to understand what was at stake.

"Family and friends will surprise you."

For many years, Andi prescribed to the thought that when she made it in the FBI and accomplished her goals, friends and family would support her. Unfortunately, that wasn't the case in the least when it came to her mother. She hadn't spoken to her in a few weeks because of her new position in the task force. Her father and brother supported her, but getting a positive response from her mom was hard. It'd been that way all her life, and she still didn't know why she felt like her mother treated her differently than her brother.

Victor asked, "Where to now?"

"Leslie's last known address." Andi typed it in the GPS and felt her phone vibrate.

Hilary: *Levi said you accused him of being a terrorist.*

Andi: *I can't talk now.*

Hilary: *You had no right.*

Andi: *Hilary, that's not how it happened.*

Hilary: *Then tell me the truth because my best friend wouldn't act so cold.*

Andi's eye twitched. The car stopped, and she lifted her head to see Victor removing his seat belt and glancing at the apartment building.

Victor repeated, "Family and friends will surprise you."

Andi nodded, closing the text thread and climbing out of the SUV. They jogged up the stairs and opened the door into the hallway of the building.

Victor ran his finger along the names on the mailboxes, noticing "L.W" printed on number ten.

"Tenth floor," Victor announced.

Andi ran a hand over her holster. "Should we take the elevator or stairs?"

"Stairs," Victor confirmed as tenants came and went off the elevator.

Five minutes into climbing the stairs, Andi felt a sense of dread. Each time that feeling came, something bad happened.

Victor made it to the door and pressed a finger to his lips for her to be quiet while he opened it. He looked down the hallway, left and right. "Clear," he whispered.

Andi came around to take the lead and removed her gun while walking slowly down the corridor. Victor came to the right of her and lightly knocked on the door.

Andi and Victor covered themselves as gunshots rang out.

"I'm not going in!" Leslie yelled.

Another bullet went through the door, and Andi returned fire.

"Are you good?" Andi shouted to Victor.

"Fine!"

Two more gunshots blasted.

Andi shot back into the apartment and listened as the bullets paused. She peeped through the hole one of the bullets had made and saw Leslie tamper with his gun. Leaning back, she kicked the door in with her gun drawn.

"Drop the gun!" Andi screamed.

"Fuck!" Leslie put the shotgun on the floor.

"Kick it away from you and put your hands in the air."

Victor watched her back with his gun drawn while Andi removed her handcuffs. A few seconds went by as other tenants came to investigate the gunshots.

"Stay back! FBI." Victor held his badge in the air.

"Leslie Witherberg?" Andi demanded.

"I'm not talking to you."

"You just shot at federal agents. I suggest you cooperate." Andi glared at him.

Leslie smirked and averted his gaze.

"Where's the next bomb?"

"Don't know what you're talking about."

Chapter Six

Andi and Victor helped Leslie slide into the back of the SUV as reporters, ambulances, and the fire department all showed up.

"Agent Easton, is it true you've arrested the suspect involved with the two bombings?" Julie, a GNG news reporter, asked.

"No comment."

"Surely you can give the citizens some type of update."

"No comment."

"Interesting how you're quiet on the subject but have close ties to the Hawthorn family."

Andi felt she was trying to have a gotcha moment. "No comment," she repeated for the third time, climbing into the front seat.

Victor shook his head, driving back to headquarters.

Andi watched through the rearview mirror as the reporter stared at their vehicle as they drove off. "She's going to be a problem."

"All of them are," Victor replied.

Thirty minutes later, Andi locked Leslie's wrists to the table in the interrogation room and removed her jacket, taking a seat in front of him. She flipped open his file. "Leslie Witherberg, born and raised in DC."

Leslie ignored her.

"Leslie, the only thing you should be worried about is whether you'll get to say goodbye to your family," Victor stated.

"I had nothing to do with any bombings," Leslie muttered.

"Why do we have you on photo delivering a video with Senator Hawthorn to the Hawthorn home?" Andi asked.

"I get paid to deliver." Leslie shrugged.

"DC Flower Galore has been closed for the past two years."

"I work freelance."

"Under their brand, and you expect me to believe that?"

"Look, I bought a van like that from some guy."

"What guy?"

"I don't remember."

"Leslie, you realize we hold all the cards. I'm doing this interview to help you."

"You're all the same."

"Agent Easton to you."

"I have nothing to hide, Agent Easton."

"So tell me about the video," Victor questioned

Andi quickly followed up with another one. "What is your relationship to Levi Baldwin?"

"My job was to deliver the tape, I'd get money, and keep the van."

"So you didn't buy the van."

"No."

"A lie. Leslie, this isn't going in your favor." Andi sat back in the chair.

"He asked if I wanted to make some extra money to take the van and deliver the tape."

"Who?" Andi shouted.

"Marlin Hawthorn!" Leslie screamed.

Andi and Victor paused in astonishment. "What else?"

Leslie drew a deep, audible breath. "That's all I know."

Director Morgan poked his head in and waved for them to come out.

"Sir, we're not finished," Andi informed him.

"You are for now. We just got another call," Morgan expressed.

"Where?"

"A school." Morgan clenched his fists.

Andi's eyes widened in surprise.

"A school," Victor murmured.

"We need to get over there."

"They gave us ten minutes before it'll go off but didn't tell us where it's placed."

"What about Senator Hawthorn?"

"He's dead, Andi."

"But—"

"I'm sorry. His body was dropped off in front of the school."

Andi covered her mouth in shock. "They didn't give us enough time."

"I agree, but we need to save those kids."

"Keep someone on Leslie and get Marlin Hawthorn

down here." Andi grabbed her keys, phone, and gun and ran out of the office with some of her team.

The team piled into trucks, geared up in vests and protection. The bomb squad led the way to the school. As soon as they approached, Andi noticed a news van behind them. She cursed under her breath and closed her eyes to control her anger.

"We have a guest." Andi pointed at the mirror for the team to check, and they all groaned in frustration and anger.

"Have the police block them off," Victor commanded through the radio.

Sirens aired to get them through traffic lights, and Andi wondered if things would ever be the same in the city after the scares they'd dealt with lately.

Her phone rang, and she lifted it to see the blocked number. It must be them. "A school?" Andi seethed.

"I had to get your attention, Agent Easton."

"Tell me who I'm speaking to."

"My demands were clear, and you decided to ignore them."

"Releasing terrorists will never happen."

"Then more bloodshed will occur."

"What's your relationship with Leslie?"

"Oh, Leslie happens to be expendable."

"Marlin Hawthorn?"

The phone went silent.

"How much is Marlin paying you?"

"Money isn't my motive, Andi. This country is going to learn."

"By giving two terrorists freedom?"

"Look at it as a favor to me."

"Marlin?"

"Sorry, not Marlin, but I will say he didn't know we'd kill his brother."

Andi held the phone on speaker. "If we release them, will you tell us where the bomb is?"

"Time is running out. You'll have to find it, Agent Easton." He dropped the call.

Andi slammed her hand on the dashboard. "I want Marlin arrested now!"

Victor checked the time on his watch. "Already being done."

A few minutes later, the team climbed out of the trucks and started directing traffic, cutting people off the block. One agent came with a map of the school and placed it on top of the SUV, and they scanned over the documents as the principal walked out with a few teachers.

Victor introduced himself, then Andi.

"Principal Hudson." Andi extended her hand.

"Yes, I got a call about a bomb threat," Principal Hudson responded.

"We received a tip about a possible threat and don't want to cause any alarm."

"Does this have anything to do with the other bombings?" Principal Hudson worried.

Andi explained, "At this time, we are still gathering information. For now, we need to get to work."

"No one is to go in or out. We only have a small window," Victor instructed.

"Oh, my God." Andi put a hand to her chest. "It's already been a minute."

"Get the team in there and start to pull kids out."

Andi reached for her phone as it rang.

"All of this can end if you release my men."

"We have a deal," Andi hurriedly answered.

The voice spat, "You're lying."

"I've no reason to lie. Tell us where the bomb is, and I'll arrange the release." Andi snapped her finger and pointed to her phone.

Victor muttered to the team to trace the call.

He demanded, "I want them unescorted with a camera and phone attached."

"Sure, no problem."

Andi looked around the onlookers piled up, including news reporters, and saw one tall figure with a phone to his ear turned away while everyone else was facing forward. Andi scratched the back of her neck and sent a signal with her chin toward the crowd. Victor caught on and faced the people behind the barrier. He scanned the crowd and saw the man with a phone to his ear and something in his hand.

"Come with me, and you two take the left, right spread out, but don't cause interruption."

Victor motioned with his hand for Andi to keep him talking.

Andi moved in closer to the crowd while still on the phone.

"You'll have one hour to release my men."

"You never told me why."

"Obviously, you know nothing about loyalty."

"Loyalty?" she repeated.

"Ted Hawthorn wasn't loyal to Marlin and wanted to sell his company."

"Sell to who?"

"I wanted my men to be free, and he wanted Ted removed."

Andi watched the anger appear on his face as he talked.

Victor placed his hand on his gun, ready to attack.

"Comes down to money for some and freedom for others."

"We are alike, Agent Easton."

"No, I'm nothing like you. Put your hands in the air, and don't move." Andi held her gun on the back of his head.

Victor snatched the alarm out of his hand and ran to the bomb squad as other officers handcuffed and turned the man around to face Andi.

He smiled. "Nice to meet you, Agent Andi Easton."

"Who are you?"

"Gregor Vlahos, and we're just getting started."

The officer walked him to the cruiser and pushed him into the back seat.

Victor sprinted back to her. "We got it defused."

"The bomb is completely disabled?"

"Yeah, and the kids have no clue."

"To distract them, let them watch a movie."

Andi gazed at Gregor in the back seat. He turned to face her and grinned.

"Agent Easton, do you have a comment on what took place here today?" Julie's fingers gripped the microphone, waving for her cameraman to aim at Andi.

Andi blocked the camera from her face. "No."

"The public deserves to know."

"A statement will be made when the time is right."

Andi left her dumbstruck and marched back to the G-ride. She shut the door, covering her face to gather her thoughts and calm her anxiety.

"Marlin, what have you done?" Andi whispered to herself.

* * *

Andi slammed papers on the desk and sipped from her coffee after a long afternoon of cat-and-mouse games. Gregor was set up in one room, and Marlin—with his lawyer—came in on edge after he was arrested at his home and was in another room. Hilary had called and messaged back-to-back, but Andi avoided her.

Victor shoved a file folder on top of his desk, removed the top, and started to pull out its contents.

"Is that everything about Gregor?"

"One Gregor Vlahos from Greece with ties to countries on the terrorist list.

"Let me guess, those who want to destroy our country."

"Ding, ding."

"Somehow, I have to tell my best friend her father helped to kill her uncle."

Victor picked up his coffee and nodded in response. "You can't take on their problems, Andi."

"Easy for you to say."

"Marlin has business ties to a lot of companies offering him more money than he could imagine. All they wanted in return was their men to be released."

"So they can go off and figure out a way to kill us again."

"It seems Marlin wanted the bill to die in Congress. He has text messages back and forth with Ted."

"Ted wouldn't take a bribe from him." Andi read the messages.

"Levi isn't involved to the extent like Marlin." Victor showed her the bank trail from Marlin to Gregor.

"Hilary and Dee will still be devastated."

"Easton, Conway, they're ready." Director Morgan waved from outside the interrogation room.

Andi placed her coffee on the desk, picked up her jacket, slid her arms inside, and pulled herself together. She saw the smug look on Marlin's face, without remorse, and shook her head.

"Mr. Hawthorn," Andi muttered.

Marlin responded, "Andi, I'm truly disappointed in you."

"In me," Andi chuckled.

Marlin sat with hands clasped together and legs crossed. "Yes, all of this is a misunderstanding."

Andi slammed her hands down and hovered over the table.

"Andi," Director Morgan called her name.

"You are pathetic."

"Dear, you need to realize all I did was business. All of my paper is legit."

"Kids could have died," Andi yelled and kicked her chair back.

"Director Morgan, if you don't control your agent, I will have to ask her to leave," Marlin's lawyer explained.

"Hilary looked up to you."

Marlin dropped the smile and glared.

"Innocent people have died because of your greed."

"Everything I've done is above board, documents signed off correctly."

"Doesn't matter how you place it in a box. You still had your brother killed," Andi said.

"What proof do you have?"

"Gregor confessed already," Victor blurted.

Marlin leaned toward his lawyer and whispered.

His lawyer replied, "Mr. Vlahos is a well-known terrorist."

"It's a matter of life in prison or death penalty—"

"Now, hold on." His lawyer raised his hand to interrupt.

Chapter Seven

They questioned Gregor Vlahos hours into the night and looked into his past. Andi finally left the office drained physically and mentally from the lies she'd uncovered. She waved good night to Victor and Director Morgan, then shut her door and closed her eyes before she decided to get on the road.

The radio clock showed midnight, and Andi was ready to get home to her bed. She held her badge up to the guard, who opened the gate for her to exit and pull onto the streets heading toward her home. Andi pulled up to the traffic light and tapped her fingers against the steering wheel to keep herself awake. When the light changed green, she nudged forward.

There was a sudden crunch of metal, and her Honda swerved. She was hit on the passenger side and gripped the wheel to avoid hitting another vehicle. In a haze, she saw two gunmen wearing ski masks jog over. She unbuckled her seat belt, pushed the door open, and fell to the ground as bullets littered the vehicle. Andi felt blood on her head as other cars continued to pass by. She reached for her gun, and through the blood seeping down her forehead, she shot one gunman in the leg.

He yelled as the other gunman ran toward the driver's side and saw it was empty. He looked in the rest of the car, then up to see Andi running down the block.

Bullets ricocheted around her and Andi turned briefly to send shots back at him. She scanned the block before running toward an apartment building. Slipping behind a guest pulling through the gate, she sprinted inside and saw a security guard.

Out of breath, she demanded, "I need to use your phone."

"What's going on?" he questioned.

"There's—"

A bullet went through his head. Andi ran around the desk and shot back at the suspect.

"Awwwh!"

Andi checked the guard's pulse and felt nothing. He was gone, and she knew it was her fault.

"Ugh!"

Andi heard the cry of pain, then lifted the phone and dialed.

"Conway."

Andi's breaths were slow, and her head pounded. "Victor, I need you to meet me at... Thirty-six and Adams."

"Andi?"

"Yeah, it's a shoot-out. And send an ambulance to a car crash down the block."

Andi dropped the phone, walked over to the suspect slowly, and kicked his gun away. "Who sent you?"

"Fuck you." He reached down to his ankle, and she saw another gun.

"Don't do it!"

"This is for Vlahos!" he yelled.

Andi shot him over and over again.

Sirens blared, and seconds later, Victor arrived with backup and saw Andi bent over at the guard station.

"Andi."

"Victor." Andi let him take the gun out of her hands.

"It's me. I got you."

"I need to get back to the bureau."

"No, a hospital is what you need."

Victor helped her into the back of the ambulance, and she lay down as they started to check her over.

"Vlahos had this planned all along."

"Relax, I got the team on it now. They must have been following you after you left."

"They killed a guard."

"We need to put an oxygen mask on you," an EMT said.

"Victor, stay."

"You're stuck with me," Victor answered and patted her hand.

The ambulance drove from the scene and headed to the hospital as more police came upon the crash site and apartment building.

* * *

Two days later, Andi shook hands with the doctor after she was handed her discharge papers, and Victor waited to take her home. The door opened to her parents and brother with balloons.

"Andi, they're letting you go?" her dad asked.

"It's just bruises, and I can rest at home."

"Are you sure?" her brother challenged.

"Andi's breathing and blood pressure are under control. She's more than ready to be out of here," the doctor joked.

"She wouldn't have been here if she had a different job," her mother quipped, and the laughter stopped.

"Victor, you remember my parents, Jed and Paula Easton, and my brother, Aaron." Andi motioned between the three.

"Nice to meet you." Victor extended his hand to her dad and brother. Her mom rolled her eyes and ignored him.

Jed chastised, "Not today, Paula."

"Mom, if you're going to be negative, it could have waited for me when I came for family dinner," Andi challenged.

Paula sat the balloons on the chair. "Andi, don't start with me."

Andi avoided her glare. "Victor, can you drop me off at home?"

"Um, sure."

"We can take you, sis," Aaron said.

"I'll call you later, Aaron."

"You had us driving up here for nothing," Paula spat.

"Paula, let me talk to you outside," Jed grumbled.

All heads turned around as Whitney entered, and Andi knew things could escalate even further between her brother and Whitney.

Whitney joked, "I feel like I'm late to the party."

"Whitney," Aaron murmured, and she ignored him.

"Hey, girl." Andi took the flowers out of her hands.

"How are you feeling?" Whitney investigated.

"Better. Victor's taking me home."

"Do you need help with anything?" Whitney scanned the room.

Andi picked up her purse, and Victor took some of the flowers from the team off the table.

"Andi, call us when you make it home," Jed requested, kissing her forehead.

"I promise." Andi ignored her mother's frown, hugged her brother goodbye, and walked out with Whitney and Victor.

Whitney pressed for the elevator to arrive.

"Are you going to ignore the tension with your mom again?"

"Yep."

"Andi."

"Not now, Whitney. You know she's always been angry with me."

Victor held his hand out to hold the doors from closing, and Andi and Whitney stepped to the back. "Always like how?"

"I could never do right in her eyes."

"I think she worries about her little girl," Whitney answered.

"Let's drop it, please."

Victor informed, "Well, on another note, Ted Hawthorn's funeral is being televised."

"Are you going?" Andi inquired.

"Probably not."

"Yeah, I doubt they want me there since I arrested Marlin." They left the elevator, walked through the waiting room, and out to his car at the entrance. Whitney helped her climb in the front seat and bent down with her head stuck in the window.

"I'll meet you at your place."

"You don't have to babysit me."

"As your best friend, I think we need to catch up."

Andi released a sigh. "Fine. If you really want to be my best friend, grab my favorite foods."

"Wine and Chinese food." Whitney held up a thumb.

Andi chuckled as Victor started the car, and Whitney backed up, watching him pull off.

An hour later, Whitney pushed the door open with bags of food, and Andi helped her, taking some of the weight from her hands.

"How much did you order?" Andi peeked in the bag.

"Enough for dinner and breakfast tomorrow."

"That's a lot. Are we expecting someone?"

Whitney placed the bags on the counter and opened the fridge to grab bottles of water.

"I figured Victor was staying for dinner."

Andi picked up two plates from the cabinet. "He had to get back to the office."

"He's cute." Whitney winked.

"No."

"What?" Whitney feigned innocence.

Andi pointed her finger at Whitney.

"My partner and nothing more."

Whitney jested, "Girl, you are so boring."

"I like my boring life."

Andi released her hair from the bun and rolled up her sleeves, filling her plate as Whitney poured them a glass of wine.

Whitney sat alongside her on the couch. "How are you really? It's scary what you've gone through."

"Honestly, I feel better now that we've caught the people."

"Girl, I can't imagine the work you do on a daily basis."

"Sometimes it's rewarding, and sometimes it can cause me to rethink, but I love helping people."

"Well, next time, don't scare us."

"Noted."

Whitney picked through her food and cleared her throat.

Andi peeked at her through her hooded eyes. "Say it."

"Have you talked to Hilary?"

"No. I said if I go to the funeral, it will cause chaos."

"She's upset now but needs you as a friend."

"Press is camped outside of their family home."

"Think about it and decide later."

Whitney and Andi clinked glasses, drank their wine, and continued catching up on the past few days they'd missed.

Chapter Eight

The bars locked after Andi stepped in, and she thanked the guard for assisting. Gregor had a small smirk on his face and waited for her to take a seat. She removed her jacket and laid it on the back of the chair, then sat across from him.

"Agent Easton, good to see you looking well."

"Surprised?"

"Why is that?"

"You sent your men to kill me."

"If I wanted that to happen, you'd be dead."

"So what was the point?"

He shrugged. "They didn't follow directions correctly."

"Killing a federal agent is a crime, even an attempt."

"I do apologize."

"Why did you call me here?"

"We're alike, you know."

"I'm nothing like you."

"We both love our country."

"I don't kill people in the name of my country."

A twitch came across his face. "How old are you?"

"Old enough to know right from wrong," she replied.

He grinned. "There's still time for you to look beyond the surface of what they show you."

"I came down here for a lecture?"

He clasped his hands together. "All things are believable, Agent Easton. You think they put you in this position because you're top of your class?"

Her head lifted at that.

"I've watched you for months, your entire time."

"Why?"

"Because you'll be the one who has to understand that the system is broken, and you'll get caught in the middle."

"Middle of what? Stop talking in riddles!"

"That badge can help or hinder."

Andi touched her badge and looked back at him. She laughed. "You can't manipulate me, Gregor."

Gregor leaned forward. "Our meeting was destined."

Andi rose out of her seat and grabbed her jacket. "You'll be destined to life in prison." She turned and started out of the room.

"Andi," he called, and she froze. "Tell Jed I said hello."

Andi whirled with a frown, stomped toward him, and gripped his collar. "How do you know my father's name?"

She tightened her hands around his throat as he laughed, and guards entered the room to interrupt the situation.

"Agent Easton!" Director Morgan yelled.

Andi released her hands and stood back in shock.

"Like I said, you'll become one of them in time." Two guards helped him to stand and escorted him out of the room.

* * *

Andi parked, sat back in her chair, and stared at the reporters that clamored to get close-up shots of family and friends entering the rotunda. Even though Ted Hawthorn was well-liked by all sides, for the family to allow the public to say goodbye meant extra security would be needed.

Andi climbed out of the car and slipped her hands into her pockets, keeping her head down to avoid cameras. People lined up, waiting to get a look at the closed casket. The sun shined bright, and signs were held up giving prayer to the family as more limousines of political figures and celebrities arrived.

"Agent Easton, any comments on today's activities?" Julie shoved the microphone in her face.

"Today is about the family, Julie."

"We hear that Gregor Vlahos has long-held ambitions to infiltrate American politics."

"Excuse me." Andi tried to walk around her, but Julie blocked her.

"Are you afraid to tell the public the truth?"

"What truth is that?"

"The government is hiding that a school was almost blown up with children inside," Julie announced.

Andi ignored her statement. "Again, I have a funeral to attend."

Most of the family sat up front, and Andi thought it best to sit in the back to avoid drama. She saw Victor wave his hand for her to sit next to him in the second to last row.

"How long have you been here?" Andi whispered.

"About ten minutes," Victor answered.

Former senators talked about Ted at the podium, then Levi and Hilary. Andi and Hilary caught eye contact, and she dropped her head in shame when Hilary rolled her eyes.

"Did you see that?" Victor muttered.

"Hopefully, the cameras didn't catch on."

"She's pissed at the wrong person."

"Just ignore."

"Normally, I'd say talk it out, but it doesn't look like she wants to talk with you."

"Her father's in jail, and her uncle is dead. No one else to blame but me."

Victor gripped her hand and squeezed. "None of this is your fault."

"Thanks."

The service went on for another hour before everyone dispersed. Andi started to leave with Victor when someone snatched her by the back of her elbow and pushed her around.

"You have some nerve," Hilary barked.

"Hilary, not here." The stares made Andi uncomfortable.

Hilary raised her hand and slapped Andi across the face.

In response to the loud gasps, Levi reached for Hilary, and Victor removed his handcuffs.

"No, Victor, it's okay."

"She just hit an agent," Victor commented.

"I don't want you anywhere near my family," Hilary gritted through her teeth.

"Hilary, please understand I did my job."

"As my best friend, your loyalty is to my family," Hilary snarled.

Andi saw people with their phones out videoing and thought it best to end the conversation. "I'm not about to fight with you here."

"If you come near me again, I'll have you arrested for harassment," Hilary snapped.

Hilary's mom comforted her as she wept in her arms, then strolled around Andi to their awaiting limo.

Victor murmured, "Don't take it personally."

"Easy for you to say."

"Some of the guys and I are going for a drink."

"I think I've had enough of crowds."

"If you change your mind, we're going to Billy's."

"Thanks, Victor."

Andi marched back to her car with her head down to avoid attention. She hopped in and started to head home but found herself outside of Billy's Bar and Grill. Andi let out a breath, turned her car off, and stepped out. She glanced around the area and felt a sense of peace when she reached the door of the bar. Silence became no more when she saw her team sitting together in a booth, laughing. Andi smiled at a few officers she'd known for a while, strolled over to the booth, and took a seat.

"Finally decided to come out with the little people," Victor joked and took a swig of his beer.

"I know my presence was missed."

"This guy wanted to go to your house and bang on your door to get you to come outside," Elliot jested.

Andi waved him off. "I'm used to Victor being an asshole."

The waitress dropped another round of beers on the table.

"How's Hilary doing?" Carl questioned.

"Not good."

"Never easy when a family member is taken away." Carl picked up some pretzels and tossed them in his mouth.

"True, and I didn't know I would become the punching bag."

"Things got personal."

"They did, but we're here to celebrate your engagement." Andi clapped Ryan on the back.

"He's off the market. No more strip joints," Carl teased, and the entire table burst into laughter.

"Maybe your fiancée will let you have a bachelor party at a strip club," Victor exclaimed, and Andi couldn't do anything but shake her head at the guys she worked alongside. Even though people might think she was stuck up or came from money, she was extremely down to earth.

Everybody looked around as a phone rang. Andi felt her pocket, removed her phone, and answered. Complete silence engulfed her for a few seconds.

"Hello?" Andi called out.

"Agent Easton."

A voice she didn't expect to hear again stopped her in her tracks. "Gregor?"

Her entire team paused at her words.

"I hope you didn't forget about me."

"How are you calling me?"

"Told you I have my ways."

"Why are you calling me?"

"I wanted to send my condolences."

"Condolences?"

"Oh, you hadn't heard?"

"Heard what?" Andi whipped around in the direction of the door, and her team came up behind her.

"Such a young life struck so short."

"Young life?"

"Sad, really."

"I'm going to hang up."

"Before you do, make sure you send my prayers to Dee Hawthorn."

Andi's heart dropped. "Hilary."

"So sad to lose your husband, brother-in-law and child in a short span of time."

Andi's mouth dropped open, and the phone fell to the ground.

Victor stooped in front of her face and snapped his fingers. "Andi, what's wrong?"

"Hilary."

"What about Hilary?"

"She's dead," Andi mumbled.

Victor reached down and picked up the phone.

"Hello? Hello!" Victor yelled into the phone; no one answered back.

Chapter Nine

"Tragically, we're reporting on the suicide of Hilary Hawthorn, the daughter of Dee and Marlin Hawthorn," GNG news station reported.

Andi sat on her couch with the same coverage playing on repeat. A day after the funeral and receiving that phone call, she locked herself in the apartment, not answering calls or doors. She couldn't believe her best friend was dead and had hated her. The many years played back in her head, from her and Hilary doing dress-up, going out together, and wanting to achieve their goals in life.

Dee told her that Hilary had overdosed on pills, and Levi was distraught. She'd tried to get Hilary to talk to him when she first started acting weird when her father got arrested.

The front door opened to Whitney and Victor.

"Andi." Whitney sat next to her on the couch.

Andi turned her head to face Whitney.

"We've been worried about you."

"Whitney," Andi mumbled.

"Everybody's been calling."

"I'm fine."

"No, you're not."

"I'm sorry about your friend, Andi. If you need time, Director Morgan will understand."

"Do you have a new case?"

Whitney and Victor looked at each other.

"Work can wait, Andi."

"Whitney, I'm fine. I promise."

"Hilary was my friend too. You need time to grieve."

"I need to get back to work. Life moves on. I had to do my job, and I did it well."

Victor and Whitney held a perplexed look.

"What are you talking about, Andi?"

"Gregor's only the beginning. There'll be more like him."

"Wait, Gregor Vlahos?" Victor remarked.

Andi slipped her feet into her shoes, picked up the remote, and turned the TV off. "As an FBI agent, I had a duty to protect. Hilary didn't understand my job is bigger than me. Gregor made me see we walk the line, and at any moment, they're waiting for us to drop the ball."

"I understand, but you need to spend time with your family."

"I'm doing this for my family." Andi picked up her gun and slipped it into her holster. "Any new cases come across your desk?" Andi locked her door behind Whitney and Victor as they sauntered to the elevator.

"Um, one case."

Whitney frowned. "Are you sure about getting back into work so fast?"

"Whitney, I'm fine."

Andi pressed the button over and over to the lobby.

"What's the case?"

"A body washed up on Rock Creek."

"I guess we're going diving."

* * *

"Ladies and gentlemen, we've received reports of multiple bodies uncovered at Rock Creek."

"Reports are still coming in, Julie, but we have the FBI on scene."

"Are you able to get any comment on how many or if anyone is alive?"

The camera panned around to Victor, Andi, and their team standing over the scene as body bags were loaded up. Andi soon realized the camera was pointed at them and covered her face.

"We have Terrorist Task Assessment out here, and so far, no statement."

"Ladies and gentlemen, we're GNG news and will keep you updated on all things dealing with this agency. More questions have risen from Agent Andi Easton, leading under Director Morgan," Julie spoke into the camera.

* * *

I hope you enjoyed Andi's story so far, and get ready for more cases. Also, please check out **"Agent Red-Fatal Revenge Teagan Stone Book 7"** sneak peek with a host of intertwined characters. Also, if you love mystery, suspense and thriller, check out **"Mirror of**

Lies Book 1" here https://books2read.com/u/mg-jEPx or another thriller/crime fiction **"Mirror of Lust Book 2" here** https://books2read.com/u/mVRpz2

Check out the free short here, ***"The Firm"*** https://payhip.com/b/py7S

Grab Boxset **"Agent Red 1-3"** here https://payhip.com/b/1KcxY

Sneak Peek Agent Red: Fatal Revenge Book 7

When enemies decide to plot together and bring down a friendly ally, it takes more than the team to get things under control. Will it come at a cost bigger than her job? Her family can only hope she comes home night after night, but things turn upside down when she's put in a terrible situation beyond her control.

Reading Order Teagan Stone Series

1. Agent Red-Fatal Memory Book 1
https://books2read.com/u/4j2PYX
2. Agent Red-Fatal Target Book
https://books2read.com/u/bWP8Jq
3. Agent Red-Fatal Crime Book
https://books2read.com/u/mZadZJ
4. Agent Red-Fatal Justice Book
https://books2read.com/u/mqo7wd

5. Agent Red-Fatal Enemy Book
https://books2read.com/u/bxeo1q
6. Agent Red-Fatal Death Book
https://books2read.com/u/mqwlRv

Reading Order of Mirror Series

Mirror of Lies Book 1
https://books2read.com/u/mgjEPx

Mirror of Lust Book 2
https://books2read.com/u/mVRpz2

Mirror of Danger Book 3

Mirror of Murder Book 4

What's Next?

Want to know what happens next? Follow me at the links below to catch the next release.

Thank you so much for reading, and if you enjoyed the crazy ride and decided to leave a review, we'd truly appreciate the support. Reviews are the lifeblood of the publishing world. They're read, appreciated, and needed. Please consider taking the time to leave a few words on Goodreads or BookBub.

Sign up for updates and sneak peeks at the sites below:
www.authoravasking.com
www.bookbub.com/avasking
www.goodreads.com/author/avasking
www.Twitter.com/authoravaking
www.Instagram.com/authoravasking
www.Facebook.com/authoravasking
www.304publishing.tumblr.com

Acknowledgments

I want to thank my team, which helps me behind the scenes, from my editors to my test readers and graphic designers, and the list goes on. I truly appreciate each of you for keeping me on my toes.

About the Author

Ava S. King is the debut author of thriller, mystery, suspense, and psychological crime novels.

If you want to know when the next book will come out, please visit Author Ava S. King's website at http://www.authoravasking.com, where you can sign up to receive an email for her next release.

About 304 Publishing Company

We showcase authors writing African American, interracial, women's fiction, urban romance, erotica, and contemporary romance novels, along with thrillers, suspense novels, poetry collections, and beauty & style books.

www.304publishing.com

Join our mailing list to stay updated with new releases and blog posts.